You Know It!

Gotcha!

SAMMY
the Steiger

FRANKIE
the Farmall

CODY
the Combine

Hey Dudes!

Go Team!

Awesome!

BAILEY
the Baler

KELLIE
the Combine

PETER
the Patriot Sprayer

VROOM!

Let's Do It!

Details!

SCOOTER
the Case IH Scout

TAMMI
the Tiller

EVAN
the Early Riser Planter

This book belongs to:

Name: _ _ _ _ _ _ _ _ _ _ _ _ _ _ _

Favorite food: _ _ _ _ _ _ _ _ _ _ _

Combines
with Casey & Friends

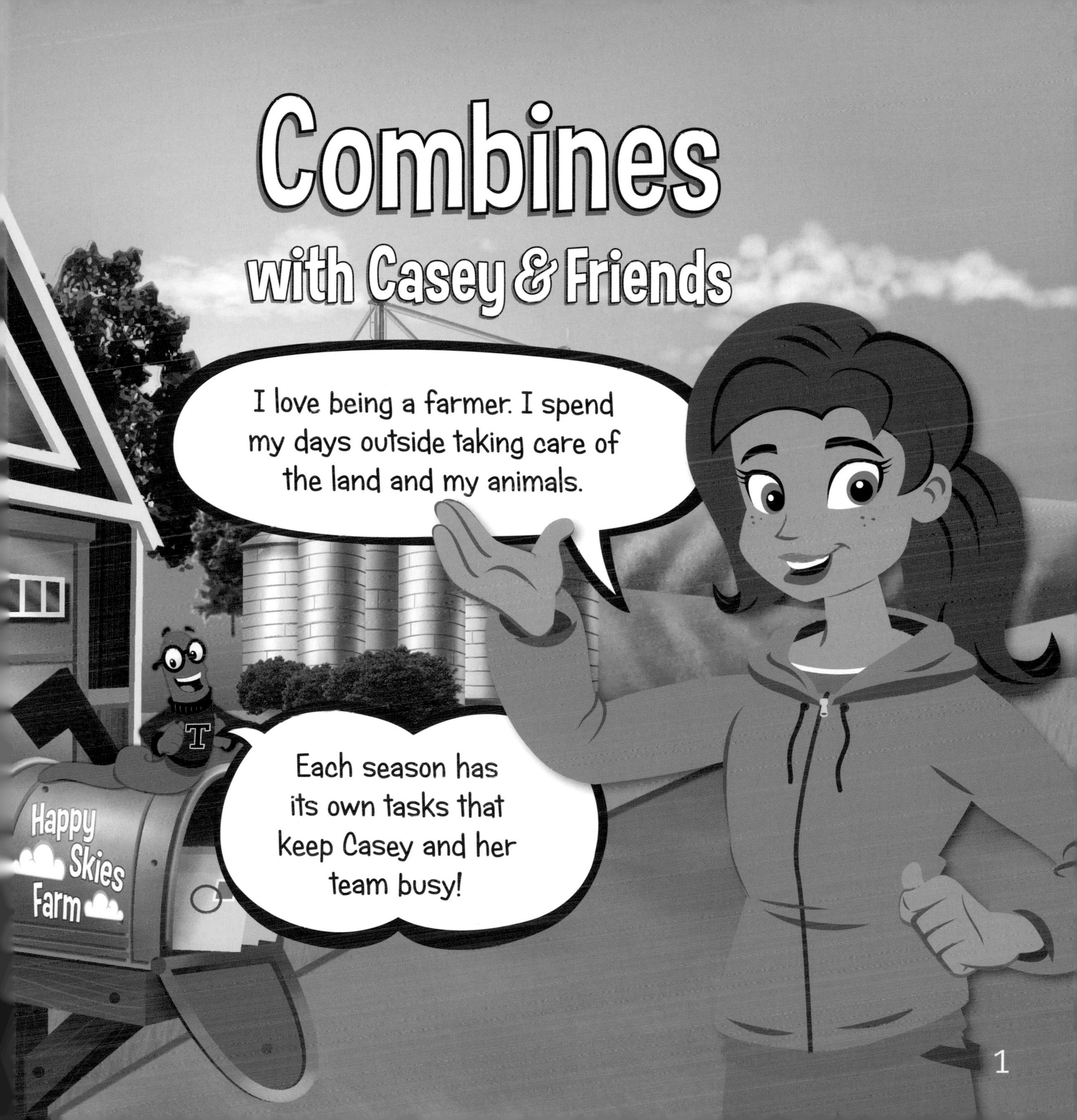

I don't stop. I can work all night.

Inventions That Changed Harvesting

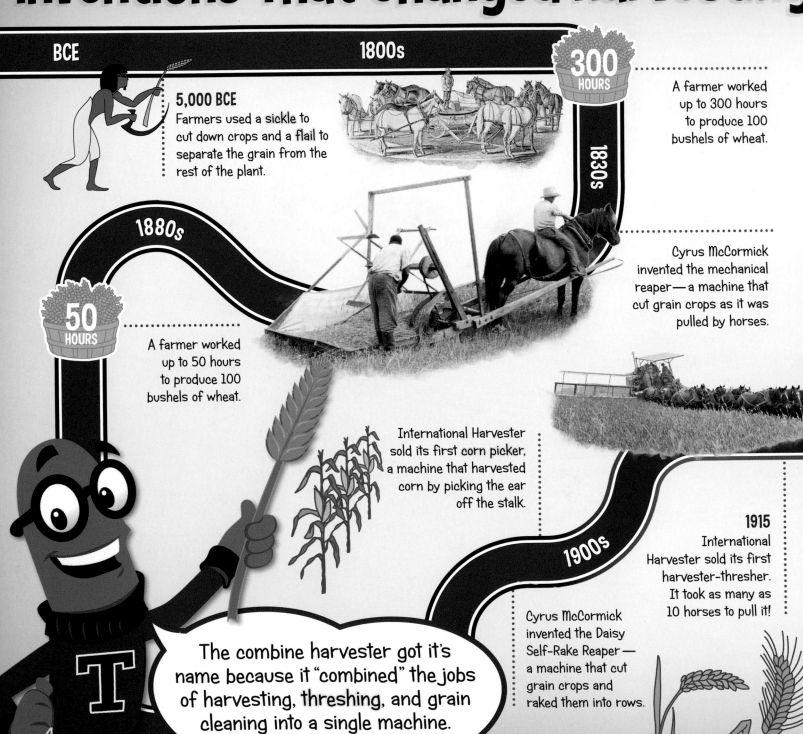

BCE

1800s

5,000 BCE
Farmers used a sickle to cut down crops and a flail to separate the grain from the rest of the plant.

300 HOURS

A farmer worked up to 300 hours to produce 100 bushels of wheat.

1830s

Cyrus McCormick invented the mechanical reaper—a machine that cut grain crops as it was pulled by horses.

1880s

50 HOURS

A farmer worked up to 50 hours to produce 100 bushels of wheat.

International Harvester sold its first corn picker, a machine that harvested corn by picking the ear off the stalk.

1900s

1915
International Harvester sold its first harvester-thresher. It took as many as 10 horses to pull it!

Cyrus McCormick invented the Daisy Self-Rake Reaper — a machine that cut grain crops and raked them into rows.

The combine harvester got it's name because it "combined" the jobs of harvesting, threshing, and grain cleaning into a single machine.

4

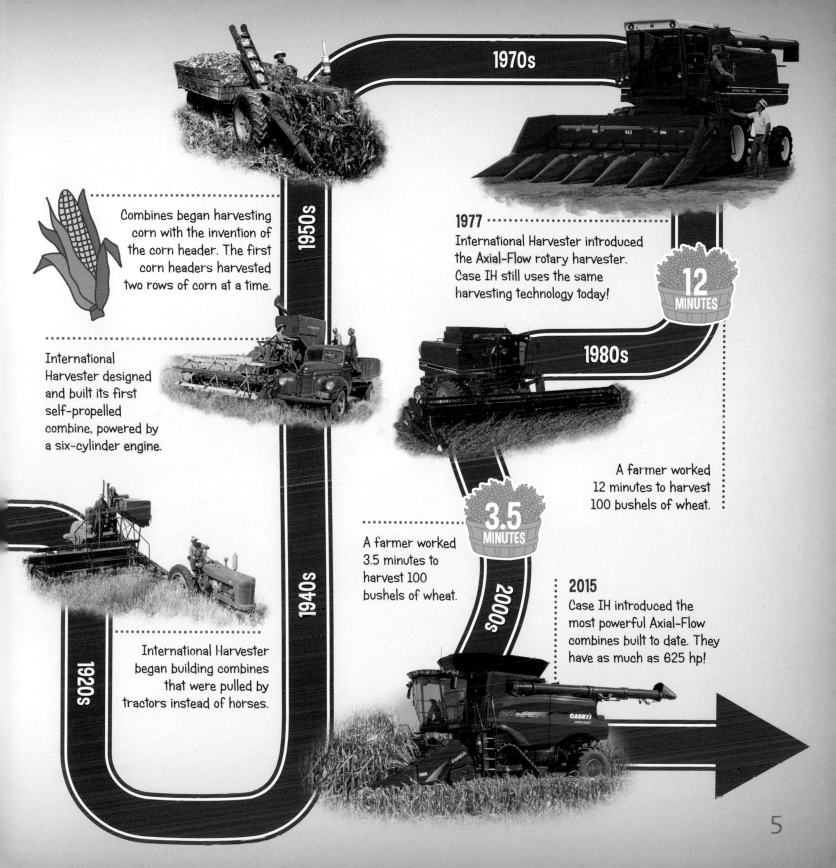

1970s

Combines began harvesting corn with the invention of the corn header. The first corn headers harvested two rows of corn at a time.

1950s

1977
International Harvester introduced the Axial-Flow rotary harvester. Case IH still uses the same harvesting technology today!

12 MINUTES

International Harvester designed and built its first self-propelled combine, powered by a six-cylinder engine.

1980s

A farmer worked 12 minutes to harvest 100 bushels of wheat.

1940s

A farmer worked 3.5 minutes to harvest 100 bushels of wheat.

3.5 MINUTES

2015
Case IH introduced the most powerful Axial-Flow combines built to date. They have as much as 625 hp!

2000s

1920s

International Harvester began building combines that were pulled by tractors instead of horses.

The Modern Combine

When it's time to harvest, I depend on Cody and Kellie. That's because each one of them completes all of the steps required to gather crops.

Cody and I do the work of three machines! We cut, separate, and clean the grain or corn.

TILLUS TALK

Bigger Is Better!

Kellie and Cody are the biggest equipment on Happy Skies Farm.

16 ft.

Kellie is more than 16 feet tall. That's as tall as stacking three horses on top of one another.

x30

Cody weighs more than 37,000 pounds. That's as much as 30 horses.

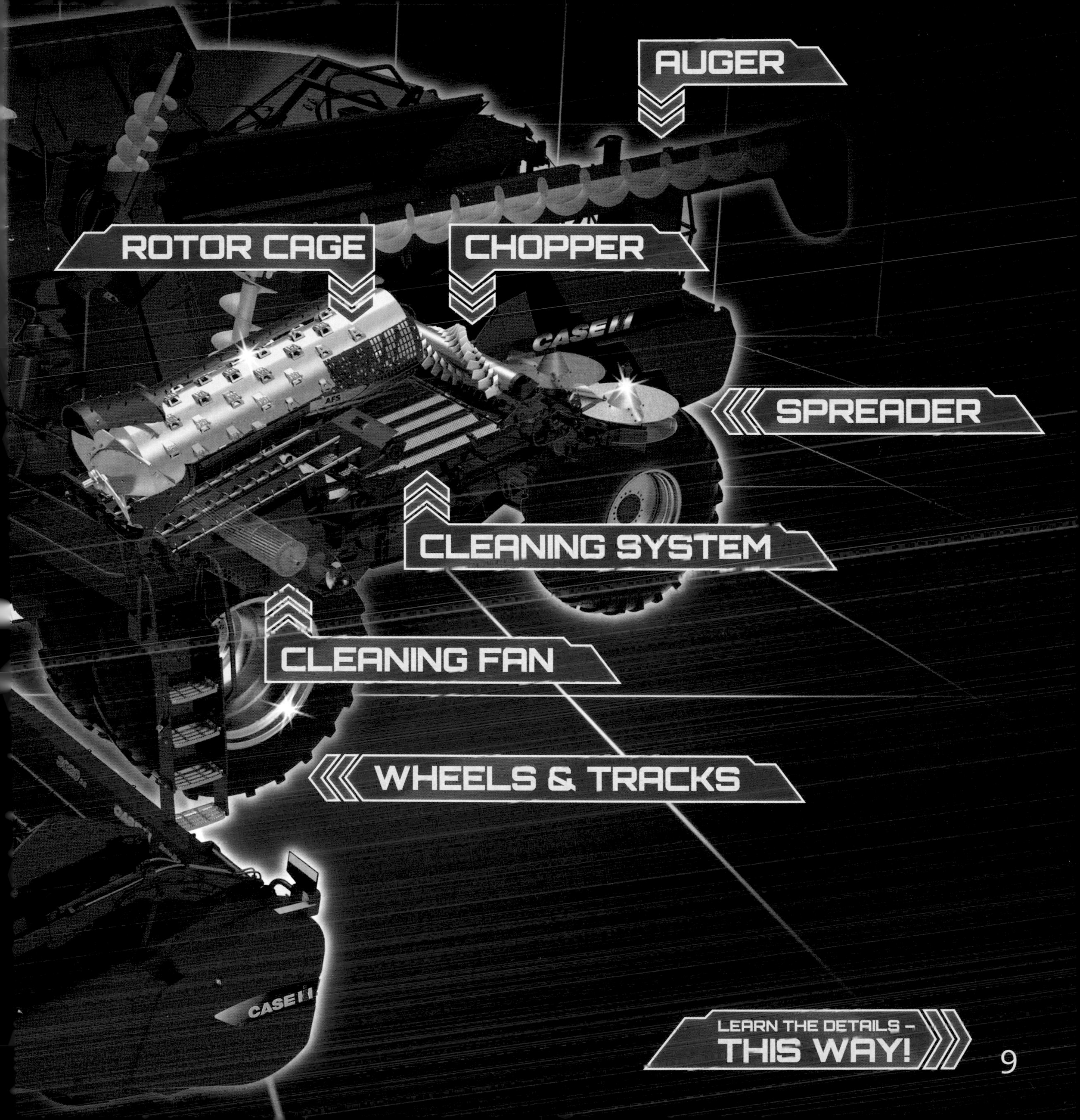

AUGER

ROTOR CAGE

CHOPPER

SPREADER

CLEANING SYSTEM

CLEANING FAN

WHEELS & TRACKS

CASE IH

CASE IH

LEARN THE DETAILS –
THIS WAY!

Reaping Grain

When my grain crops are fully grown, it's time for Kellie to reap them. As Kellie moves through the field, her header cuts the plants and feeds them into the combine's body.

10

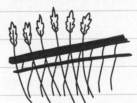

TILLUS TALK

Heading on a Wheat Adventure!

Kellie's header is designed to carefully scoop the plants into the combine without damaging them.

As the header spins...

teeth grab the plants...

and push them toward the cutter.

The plants are on a harvesting adventure!

I work just like Kellie, but my header is specially designed to harvest corn instead of grain. It cuts the tall stalks and removes the ears of corn from the plant.

TILLUS TALK

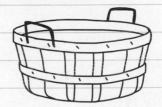

Bushels of Goodness

Harvested grain and corn are measured in bushels.

Long ago, grain and corn were measured using bushel baskets.

Over time, a bushel became a set measurement—like gallons or liters.

Cody and Kellie's grain tanks can store up to 410 bushels of harvested corn or grain!

13

Threshing and Cleaning the Crops

Once the header feeds the plants into the combine, the real work begins!

① ROTOR

As the crop spins around the rotor, the grain or corn kernels separate from the rest of the plant.

② ROTOR CAGE

When the tiny grain seeds or corn kernels separate from the plant, they fall through the openings in a cage that surrounds the rotor.

③ GRAIN PAN

The grain pan collects the seeds and small pieces of plant that fall from the rotor. The grain pan moves back and forth very quickly, forcing the grain seed or corn kernels to fall to the bottom.

④ CLEANING FAN

The cleaning fan blows the leftover pieces out of the pan. All that is left is clean grain or corn kernels!

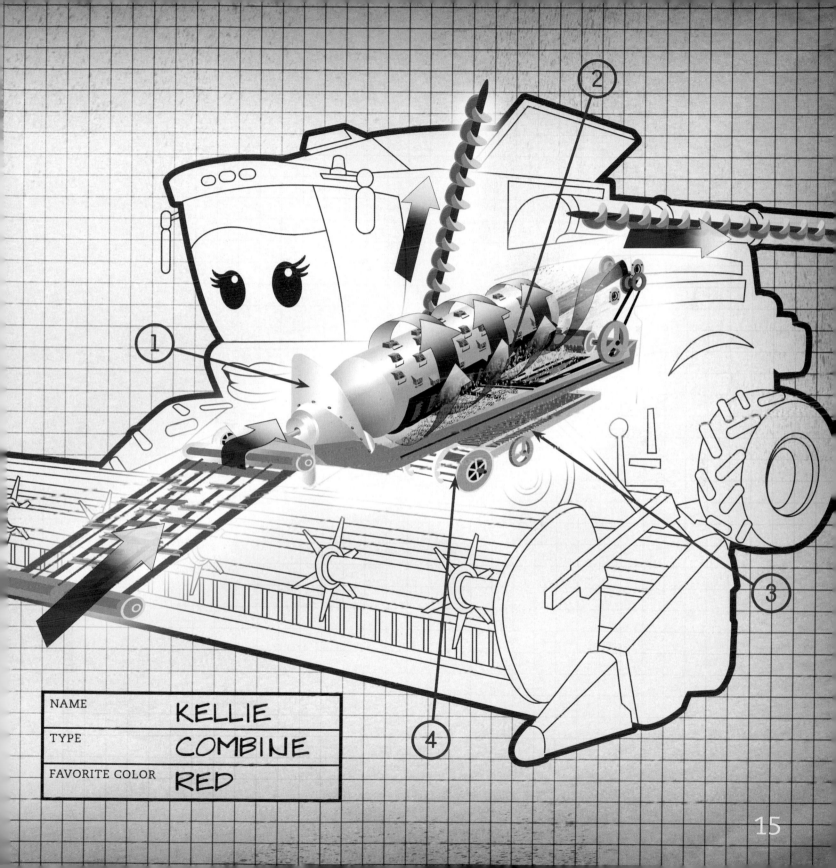

NAME KELLIE

TYPE COMBINE

FAVORITE COLOR RED

Time to Unload

⑤ GRAIN TANK

Clean grain is stored in a large tank. When the tank is full, the combine must unload it into a truck or wagon using the auger.

⑥ AUGER

The auger unfolds and moves above a truck or grain cart. The auger unloads the grain by shooting it out into the waiting container.

⑦ CHOPPER

The leftover plant material is fed through the combine to the chopper. The chopper cuts it up into tiny pieces.

⑧ SPREADER

The spreader shoots out the cut-up pieces onto the field. This protects the soil for next year's crop.

Once the grain is clean, it is ready to be stored or unloaded. And what happens to the rest of the plant? The combine makes sure that every piece of crop is used!

17

My Mission Control Center

I control my combine from its cab. It is similar to the cabs in my big tractors.

STEERING

The steering wheel controls which direction the combine moves.

WINDSHIELD

The windshield allows Casey to see all of the header while it works.

SEAT

The seat is on special springs that help keep Casey comfortable when she goes over bumps.

BUDDY SEAT

The buddy seat allows Tillus to ride along with Casey. Casey stores her water in a cooler under the buddy seat.

COMPUTER

The touchscreen computer gives Casey important information about the soil and the crop.

CONTROL CENTER

The special handle and armrest control different parts of the combine, including the header, rotor, and auger.

19

Let's Roll

Combines are very heavy, but they don't sink. That's because the wide wheels and tracks spread their weight evenly over the soil.

8240 AFS

The Future of Combines

Harvesting tools have come a long way since the sickle and flail. I wonder what the future of harvesting will look like?

It would be awesome if I could fly!

Teamwork in Harvesting

Cody and Kellie may do all the work to harvest crops, but other equipment helps, too. Tractors transfer the harvested grains and corn from the combine to waiting semitrucks that carry it to the farm or grain mill.

I pull the grain cart alongside Cody and Kellie so they can unload as they work!

TILLUS TALK

Stuck Like Glue!

Big Red follows Cody and Kellie using special technology called Advanced Farming System (AFS).

AFS allows Cody and Kellie to control how fast or slow Big Red goes.

That's important because the grain cart *always* needs to be under the auger!

What do you think would happen if Big Red went faster than Cody or Kellie?

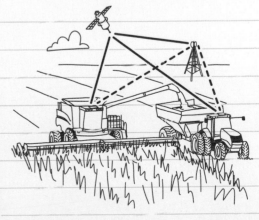

Unusual Harvesting Equipment

Cody and Kellie are my main harvesting equipment, but combines are not the only equipment that harvests crops.

COTTON
HARVESTER

SUGAR CANE
HARVESTER

COFFEE
HARVESTER

TILLUS TALK

One Combine Harvests Many Crops!

Farmers change the header to fit the crop. Using different headers allows one combine to harvest...

Alfalfa	Mustard Seed
Barley	Oats
Beans	Onion Seed
Borage	Peas
Buckwheat	Primrose
Canola	Radishes
Corn	Rice
Fescue	Rye
Flax	Safflower
Grasses	Sunflowers
Linseed	Wheat
Maize	

And that's not all! Can you think of any other types of crops a combine might harvest?

27

From Plants to Products

Match the crop to the product it makes!

Everything you eat has been harvested by equipment or by hand. But harvested crops are used for more than just food. Clothes, crayons, fuel, and some kinds of toothpaste come from plants that were harvested, too!

FLAX

RYE

SOY

SUNFLOWER

GLOSSARY

ADVANCED FARMING SYSTEM (AFS)

special technology found in Case IH combines used to help harvest crops and gather information

AXIAL-FLOW

name of the rotor technology that Case IH uses in its combines

BUSHEL

the measurement used for harvested grains and corn

CORN PICKER

equipment that harvested corn by picking the ear off the stalk

ENGINE

a machine that turns energy into motion

FLAIL

stick-like hand tool used to separate grain seeds from the rest of the plant

GRAIN CART

large wagon used for
collecting grain

HARVESTING

to gather fully grown
plants for use

SICKLE

a curved knife used
for cutting down
plants

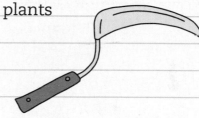

GRAIN CROP

a plant such as wheat,
rye, and barley grown
by farmers

THRESHING

the second step in
harvesting—separating the
grain seed or corn kernel
from the rest of the plant

REAP

the first step in harvesting—to
cut down fully grown plants

TRACTION

the action of gripping the
ground to stop slipping

GRAIN MILL

a place where grain is
ground into flour

FUN FACTS!

The cleaning fan in a combine blows at 65 mph!

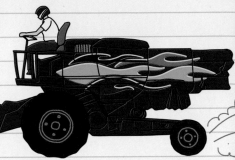

Combines race in Demolition Derby events.

One acre of wheat can produce 2,500 loaves of wheat bread!

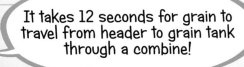

It takes 12 seconds for grain to travel from header to grain tank through a combine!

One bushel of wheat contains about one million individual grain seeds.

The word "cereal" comes from the ancient Roman goddess of grain crops—Ceres.

Corn always has an even number of rows on a cob.

Custom harvesters or cutters are people who specialize in harvesting crops for farmers.

Bob Cutter
Harvest Specialist
555-1234

32

Octane Press, Edition 1.2 (Hardcover), September 2023
Edition 1.1 (Softcover), October 2022
Edition 1.0 (Hardcover), June 2015

Library of Congress Cataloging-in-Publication Data

ISBN-13: 978-1-937747-54-1 ISBN-10: 1937747549

1. Juvenile Nonfiction—Transportation—General. 2. Juvenile Nonfiction—Lifestyles—Farm and Ranch Life.

3. Juvenile Nonfiction—Lifestyles—Country Life. 4. Juvenile Nonfiction—Concepts—Seasons

Library of Congress Control Number: 2014954286

Additional photography used with permission from The Wisconsin Historical Society p. 4 (ID24863, ID11009) and p. 5 (ID23688, ID24616, ID85076)

octanepress.com

Printed in China

Farming keeps me busy,
but I love my life!

CASEY
the Farmer

Casey depends on me for
the daily weather report!

TILLUS
the Worm

Easy Peasy!

Be Ready!

FERN
the Farmall

BIG RED
the Magnum